DANGEROUS GAMES

SUPERHERO MISSION

Sue Graves

Rising Stars UK Ltd.
7 Hatchers Mews, Bermondsey Street, London SE1 3GS
www.risingstars-uk.com

 nasen

NASEN House, 4/5 Amber Business Village, Amber Close,
Amington, Tamworth, Staffordshire B77 4RP

Published 2012

Author: Sue Graves
Series editor: Sasha Morton
Text and logo design: pentacor**big**
Typesetting: Geoff Rayner, Bag of Badgers
Cover design: Lon Chan
Publisher: Gill Budgell
Project Manager: Sasha Morton Creative Project Management
Editorial: Deborah Kespert
Artwork: Colour: Lon Chan / B&W: Paul Loudon

British Library Cataloguing in Publication Data.
A CIP record for this book is available from the British Library.

ISBN: 978-0-85769-609-0

Printed by Craftprint International, Singapore

Tom, Sima and Kojo had been to the cinema for the evening to see the latest superhero movie.

The three of them worked at Dangerous Games, a computer games company. Sima designed the games, Kojo programmed them and Tom tested them. They loved their jobs and always worked as a team. They were all good mates, too.

"That movie was amazing," said Tom. "Did you see the way the superhero destroyed those aliens? He was awesome."

"It was good," agreed Kojo, "but I thought it was a bit far-fetched in places."

"How do you mean?" asked Tom.

"Well, taking on twelve aliens single-handedly would be a bit much even for a superhero," said Kojo.

"I don't agree," said Tom. "The whole point of being a superhero is that you can do anything. It would be brilliant to be able to do things like that. I'd love it."

"Would you really?" asked Sima. "Would you really want to put yourself in that much danger?"

"You bet," said Tom.

Sima smiled. "You've just given me an idea for a new game."

"A superhero game?" grinned Tom, hopefully.

"How did you guess?" laughed Sima.

CHAPTER 2

The next day, Tom and Kojo were in the office early. They were keen to get started on the new game. Sima arrived a few minutes later. She looked really pleased with herself.

"What do you think of this?" she asked the boys, pulling a bright blue coat out of a bag. "I saw it in the window of that new clothes shop on my way here. I couldn't resist it and it was a real bargain, too."

"Yeah, it's erm … er … nice!" said Kojo.

"It's a bit bright," remarked Tom.

"It's the latest trendy colour," said Sima proudly. "It's called cobalt blue."

"Hey!" said Kojo suddenly. "You've given me an idea, Sima. Why don't we use cobalt in our new game?"

"Look, I haven't had my coffee yet," sighed Tom, "so I have no idea what you are talking about. You're going to have to explain what you mean more slowly, Kojo. Some of us aren't keeping up!"

"Cobalt is a mineral that can be found in meteorites," explained Kojo. "The superhero in our new game could be on a mission to find enough cobalt to generate power on his home planet."

"Neat," said Tom. "So what shall we call his home planet?"

Sima grinned. "How about Dakron?" she suggested.

"That's a great name," said Kojo. "But how did you think of it?"

She held up her new coat. "My coat is designed by Dakron. It sounds just like a planet to me."

"Then Dakron, it is," said Tom. "Now, Sima, do you think you can put the coat away for a few minutes and get on with some work?"

"OK guys," sighed Sima. She carefully packed her coat back into its bag. "Leave me to it and I'll soon have the designs done."

Later that afternoon, Sima showed the boys her designs.

"I went online to get some data on meteorites," she said. "Apparently, loads fall to Earth in a desert in Nevada called the Great Basin, so I've set the game there. I'm calling the game Superhero Mission."

"Cool!" said Tom.

"Our superhero's name is Indigo Jones," continued Sima. "Indigo is a shade of blue and I thought we could keep the blue theme going."

"Yeah, I like it," said Tom. "Tell us what the aim of the game is."

"Well," said Sima. "It's all quite straightforward. The players have to help Indigo find enough cobalt to open a portal to transport him and the mineral back to Dakron. The people on Dakron need the cobalt to generate power on their planet, in much the same way that we rely on fuels such as gas and oil for our power supplies on Earth. Of course, the players and Indigo have to complete the task before time runs out."

"This is going to be brilliant," said Tom. "How about if we all ..."

"... Test it for real?" interrupted Sima and Kojo together, and they burst out laughing.

The next day, Kojo programmed the game.

"It's ready for testing," he said. "We'll do it this evening when everyone else has gone home." He looked at his watch. "Time for lunch, guys," he said. "Shall we pop over to the café for something to eat?"

"Why don't we skip lunch and try out the game now?" asked Tom impatiently. "It's too long to wait until this evening."

"No way," said Sima. "I'm starving. Are you coming or not, Tom?"

"I'll be with you in a minute," said Tom. "You go on ahead. I've just got something I want to finish."

CHAPTER 3

Tom waited for Sima and Kojo to go out of the office. Then, he picked up the new game disc and loaded it onto Kojo's computer.

"I'll just give it a quick trial run," he muttered to himself. "Then I can test it again this evening with the others."

Tom touched the screen. A bright light flashed and he closed his eyes tightly. The bright light faded and he opened his eyes. He was standing in a hot desert with the sun beating down on him.

Tom rolled up his sleeves and raised his arm over his head to block out the bright sunshine.

"Welcome to the Great Basin," boomed a deep voice behind him. "But this is no time to sunbathe, you're here to give me a hand."

Tom spun round. A tall man dressed entirely in indigo blue was standing nearby. His arms were folded across his chest and he was grinning at Tom.

Indigo handed Tom a small machine.

"This is called the Cobalt Classifier — it's a mineral-tracing device," he said. "This machine can pick up even small amounts of the mineral cobalt from many miles away. I have been using it to locate new meteorites that have crash-landed here from outer space. Try it for yourself."

Tom switched on the machine and slowly scanned it across the desert. Suddenly, it made a loud beeping noise. Tom looked up at Indigo and grinned.

"Success!" said Indigo and he slapped Tom on the back.

Indigo snapped his fingers and a hi-tech quad bike rose up out of the sand. The bike's frame shimmered in the heat.

THAT BIKE IS SO COOL!

Indigo looked at his watch. "We've no time to waste," he said. "Climb aboard. We've got to get the cobalt."

Tom and Indigo got on the quad bike. Indigo flicked a switch and the machine lifted off the sand and zoomed across the desert. Tom looked down. He could see that the wheels had retracted and the machine was not touching the ground at all.

Soon, they arrived at a small crater which held the remains of a meteorite. The ground around the crater was glowing and the heat coming up from it was intense.

ISN'T IT DANGEROUS TO BE SO CLOSE TO SOMETHING LIKE THIS?

YOU'LL BE FINE, TRUST ME.

Indigo showed Tom how to extract the cobalt from the meteorite using another gadget. Everything was going really well until, suddenly, Tom heard a hissing noise behind him. He spun round and saw four aliens standing a short distance away. They were closing in on Tom and Indigo.

Without taking his eyes off the aliens, Tom tapped Indigo on the shoulder. "I think we've got company," he said.

Indigo looked up. "Oh no," he said. "The aliens must have followed me to Earth. If they get the cobalt my planet will be in grave danger. This could get really nasty, Tom. Do exactly as I say."

The aliens were getting closer and closer. Slowly, Indigo bent down and grabbed a large glowing piece of rock from the meteorite. With a small flick of his wrist, he sent the rock flying into the middle of the group. The rock travelled at such an amazing speed that flames shot out from it and the aliens scattered. Indigo ran to the bike.

GET ON THE BIKE!

Tom ran and jumped on the
bike. In less than a second,
Indigo had started up the
engine and they were hurtling
across the desert. They headed
for cover towards an outcrop of
rocks at the edge of the Great
Basin, but as the machine skidded
to a stop, Tom lost his balance
and fell to the ground.

Red-hot pain shot through Tom's leg. He blacked out.

CHAPTER 4

Meanwhile, Sima and Kojo had just got back from lunch.

"I wonder where Tom got to?" said Sima. "It's not like him to miss lunch."

Just then, Pete, the IT manager, came in with a hardware delivery for Kojo.

"Have you seen Tom anywhere?" asked Sima.

"No," said Pete, as he handed over the package. "I've just got back from the canteen for lunch and he wasn't there either."

"How odd," said Sima. She looked worried.

"I don't believe it!" Kojo said. "Look! Tom's gone into the game by himself. And it looks as if he's injured."

Kojo sat down in front of his computer.

Sima ran across the room and stared at the computer screen. Tom was lying on his side near some rocks. He wasn't moving.

Kojo began rapidly typing commands on the keyboard. "I don't understand it," he said. "The game has gone into standby mode and I can't get it to move on."

"Wait," said Sima. "That might be a good thing. If the game was still running, the amount of time left to play might be nearly gone. If we enter the game now, we could still rescue Tom and get him out before it's 'Game Over'."

"But how do we know that the game won't stay in standby mode?" asked Kojo. "We might be stuck in it forever."

Sima bit her lip. "I reckon if we go into the game it might trigger it to restart. What choice do we have? We've got to help Tom. Come on!"

Kojo and Sima touched the screen together. A bright light flashed. They closed their eyes tightly. The bright light faded and they opened their eyes.

Kojo and Sima found themselves a short distance away from Tom. They ran over to him and helped him to sit up.

Tom stirred and opened his eyes. "Where am I?" he mumbled.

Just then, Indigo appeared behind them. "Game time is running out," he said. "We've got to get the cobalt to the edge of the Great Basin to open the portal. The aliens are closing in again."

"Whether you included them or not," remarked Indigo, "I can tell you that they are here, and they are dangerous. They are threatening not only the success of my mission, but the safety of planet Earth. Now come on!"

Quickly, Sima and Kojo made a splint for Tom's leg using Kojo's belt and Sima's rolled-up sweater. Then they ran to help Indigo get the cobalt to the edge of the Great Basin.

Suddenly, Kojo spotted the aliens in the distance. They were heading for Indigo and they were covering the ground between them fast. Sima and Kojo worked even more quickly. But just as Kojo put the last piece of cobalt in place, an alien lunged at him. With a roar of anger Indigo hurled the alien into the air.

BOTH OF YOU GO! PROTECT TOM!

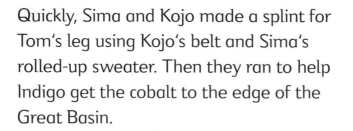

3:00

Sima and Kojo ran back to Tom. They crouched down around their injured friend, trying to protect him from the nearby aliens just as the portal opened. A blue glow started to flicker and shine above them, but then another bright light flashed and they heard the words 'Game Over!' They shut their eyes tightly.

CHAPTER 5

The bright light faded and they opened their eyes. They were back in the office.

"Did Indigo make it through the portal?" gasped Sima.

"There's only one way to find out," said Kojo. He reloaded the game. The portal was fading, but it was clear that Indigo had made it back through to his home planet. "Yes, Indigo's gone ... and so have the aliens. It's all OK."

"No it's not," replied Tom, pointing over Kojo's shoulder. "Look! One of the aliens has been left behind."

"In that case, we'll have to play the game again. But this time, we'll play it as a proper gamer, sitting at the computer. It's the only way to destroy that alien," said Kojo.

"Leave it to me," said Tom, taking up the controls.

The alien was rampaging through the state of Nevada, getting closer and closer to the Utah border. It was destroying everything in its path, and every time Tom tried to engage Indigo's power to destroy it, the alien escaped. Things were looking very serious indeed.

"It's no good, I can't destroy this thing as the game stands at the moment," said Tom. "I think the alien mutated when the game was closing last time. We need to increase Indigo's power to have any chance of destroying it. Is there anything you can do to make that happen, Kojo?"

"Yes, I can increase Indigo's powers, by fine-tuning the program a little," said Kojo, adding, "and I'll make sure he's fully equipped to destroy that alien once and for all."

Quickly, Kojo tapped out instructions on his keyboard until the screen glowed brightly and Indigo appeared again. This time he was bigger and looked more powerful than before — and he was holding the Cobalt Classifier.

"You said he would be fully equipped to destroy the alien," snapped Tom. "What good is that?"

"Just wait until you try it, Tom," said Kojo.

Tom locked his cursor onto the alien and positioned Indigo right in his path. Indigo lifted the Cobalt Classifier and took aim. A huge blue flame shot out of the barrel and hit the alien straight on. The alien exploded before their eyes and disappeared into the air in a cloud of blue dust.

Indigo raised the Classifier in a triumphant salute. "Game over," he boomed.

Then the screen faded and went blank.

"You did it, guys!" shouted Sima. "What an amazing shot."

Tom cracked his knuckles and grinned. "It was nothing!"

Just then Mr Wilson, their boss, put his head round the office door.

"There's a lot of noise coming from here this afternoon," he said. He stopped and looked at Tom's injured leg. "What on earth have you been doing?"

"Had a bit of trouble with some aliens," replied Tom truthfully.

"Don't be cheeky to me, young man," said Mr Wilson crossly. "An accident in the workplace is nothing to joke about."

Tom thought for a moment. "I tripped over a box of computer paper," he said, pointing to a box on the floor.

"You could have told me that when I first asked you," said Mr Wilson. "You'd better get down to the hospital and let them have a look at it."

"OK," said Tom, smiling politely as Sima and Kojo tried not to laugh.

Mr Wilson banged the door loudly behind him, huffing "Aliens, indeed!" as he went.

"If only he knew," giggled Sima. "If only he knew!"

GLOSSARY OF TERMS

bargain something that costs you less than you would normally pay

canteen a room in a factory, school or workplace where cheap food is served

crater a large hole on the surface of a planet caused by the impact of a meteorite

far-fetched hard to believe

generate to produce power

impact when one object hits another

meteorite(s) a piece of rock that has fallen from space

mission an important aim or job that has to be done

mode one way in which a machine can be made to work

mutate(d) to change physically and become different from others of its type

portal an entrance that leads to other places

remotely using equipment to control a machine from a short distance away

reserves supplies that can be used when needed

retracted pulled backwards or pulled inside something

splint a support, e.g. of wood or another material, to help mend a broken bone

trigger to make something happen

Quiz

1 What sort of movie had Sima, Tom and Kojo been to see?

2 What did Sima buy that she was particularly pleased with?

3 What name was given to the superhero's planet in the game?

4 Where did the name come from?

5 How was Indigo dressed?

6 How many aliens were there?

7 On what did Indigo and Tom travel across the desert?

8 How did Tom hurt himself?

9 How did Kojo check to see if Indigo had got through the portal?

10 How was the fourth alien destroyed?

ABOUT THE AUTHOR

Sue Graves has taught for thirty years in Cheshire schools. She has been writing for more than ten years and has written well over a hundred books for children and young adults.

"Nearly everyone loves computer games. They are popular with all age groups — especially young adults. But I've often thought it would be amazing to play a computer game for real. To be in on the action would be the best experience ever! That's why I wrote these stories. I hope you enjoy reading them as much as I've enjoyed writing them for you."

Answers to Quiz

1 Superhero movie

2 Cobalt blue coat

3 Dakron

4 The label in Sima's coat

5 All in blue

6 Four

7 Quad bike

8 He fell off the quad bike

9 He reloaded the game

10 Indigo shot him with the Cobalt Classifier